Olga
the Cloud

by Nicoletta Costa

Holiday House / New York

Library of Congress Cataloging-in-Publication Data
Costa, Nicoletta.
[Nuvola Olga. English.]
Olga the cloud / by Nicoletta Costa ; translated from the Italian by Grace Maccarone. — First edition.
pages cm
"First published in Italy in 2003 as LA NUVOLA OLGA by Edizioni EL S.r.l., Trieste."
Summary: Olga the cloud's wonderful day comes to an end when,
after being chased off the moon where
she was trying to nap, she has a terrible time finding
the right place to make some rain.
ISBN 978-0-8234-3051-2 (hardcover)
[1. Clouds—Fiction. 2. Rain and rainfall—Fiction.]
I. Maccarone, Grace, translator. II. Title.
PZ7.C8195Olg 2014
[E]—dc23
2013030349

This is Olga the Cloud. She's white and soft,
just like whipped cream. Here she is, happy and light,
as she drifts along the clear, blue sky.

It's a good day for Olga the Cloud.
There are so many interesting things
to see, both in the sky and on the ground.

The ocean is wonderful too.
Olga is looking at the blue waves
and the many fishes.
But suddenly . . . what a mess!
Olga gets all dirty from smoke
blowing from a ship.

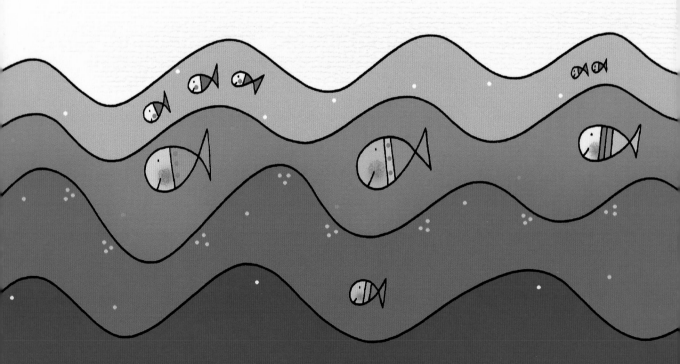

So Olga washes her face in the cool salt water,

and soon she is as clean and beautiful as before.

Olga would like to rest awhile,
but she doesn't know where.
On a rooftop? No. On a treetop? No.
They are too pointy.
On a clothesline? No. On a sailboat? No.
They are too shaky.

What about the moon?
The moon looks very comfortable.

But the moon doesn't like that idea at all.
Guests give her a headache!
So she asks Gino the Bird
to chase Olga away.
Gino shoves her gently
with the tip of his boot.

Olga drifts and drifts until she settles
over a big, sleeping cat.
"May I make a little rain?" Olga asks shyly.

The cat slowly opens his big yellow eyes.
They are so threatening that
Olga runs away at once.

Olga stops over Giacomina the Hen,
who is taking her chicks for a walk.
Olga can't wait to make a little rain.

The hen looks up and says, "You are not thinking
of doing it on my little chicks, are you?"
And so poor Olga leaves.

After drifting a while longer, she settles over
Mrs. Emilia, who's hanging her laundry.
Olga must make a little rain very soon!

But Mrs. Emilia becomes very angry.
So poor Olga is once again forced to leave.

Olga decides to stop over a sunflower field.
She really can't hold her rain any longer.
But the biggest sunflower says to her,
"It's true we are thirsty, but you are too small
to give every one of us a drink."
So Olga has to go away again.

Olga is desperate. She can't wait anymore.
She must make a little rain right now!
But thank goodness, Gino the Bird arrives
to show her where to go.

Olga finds a place where there are many, many clouds.
And all together, they make a big, wonderful rain—
and they don't have to ask anyone's permission!